Invasion of the Blobs

Paul Stewart is the very funny, very talented author of more than twenty books for children, including *The Edge Chronicles*, a collaboration with Chris Riddell.

Chris Riddell is a well-known illustrator and political cartoonist. His work appears in the *Observer* and the *New Statesman*, and he has illustrated many picture books and novels for young readers.

Both live in Brighton, where they created the Blobheads together.

All Blobheads titles can be ordered at your local bookshop or are available by post from Book Service by Post (tel: 01624 675137).

The Blobheads

Invasion of the Blobs

Paul Stewart
and Chris Riddell

MACMILLAN
CHILDREN'S BOOKS

P.S. For Joseph and Anna
C.R. For William

First published 2000 by Macmillan Children's Books
a division of Macmillan Publishers Limited
25 Eccleston Place, London SW1W 9NF
Basingstoke and Oxford
www.macmillan.co.uk

Associated companies throughout the world

ISBN 0 330 38972 6

1 3 5 7 9 8 6 4 2

A CIP catalogue record for this book is available from
the British Library.

Typeset by SX Composing DTP, Rayleigh, Essex
Printed and bound in Great Briatin by Mackays of Chatham plc, Kent

Chapter One

Billy Barnes stood in the bathroom brushing his teeth. His dad's Toffee and Avocado Surprise was clamped to the inside of his mouth like cement. It would not budge. Billy put his toothbrush down and tried to dislodge the stuff with his fingernails.

"I wish we could just have ice cream for afters, like everybody else," he muttered. But Billy knew that, like wishing it could be Christmas every day, this would never happen.

His mum's executive career left her with far too little time to cook. While his dad's job – as house-husband and main carer of Billy and Silas – left him with far too much. And this week he had completed his evening class in Creative Cookery (Advanced).

Today's menu had been Curried Strawberry Soup, then Liver and Peach Roulade, followed by the gluey pudding.

"Unnkh!" Billy grunted as a toffee impression of his top teeth clunked down into the sink.

"Bang!" came a noise from behind him.

Billy spun round, heart thumping. The noise had come from the toilet.

"The seat must have dropped down," he told himself. "That's all."

He turned back and prodded inside his mouth again. A second lump of toffee dropped into the sink. Billy was just checking that none of his teeth had fallen out when he noticed a movement in the mirror.

Billy froze. It was the toilet again. Slowly but surely, the cover and the seat were rising up. Then, as he stared open-mouthed, something appeared in the gap. Something purple and red. Something blobby. Something horribly like his dad's Pickled Grape Jelly with Raspberry Coulis – except for one thing.

It had eyes!

"Waaah!" Billy screamed.

The purple and red thing disappeared and the toilet seat banged shut. There was a muffled cry of anger followed by splashing and spluttering.

Billy turned and stared at the toilet in horror.

He leapt forwards, seized the toilet handle and pressed it down. At first there was the familiar whoosh of the toilet flushing. Then everything went horribly wrong.

The toilet began glugging and gurgling, and water gushed out from beneath the seat.

"Oh, no!" Billy gasped. The water poured down onto the floor and sloshed over the tiles.

All at once, the toilet cover flew up and out popped the thing. The thing with the blobby head and the beady eyes. The thing that Billy hoped he had only imagined.

"Waaah!" he screamed again.

The thing climbed onto the toilet rim and looked around. From behind it, there came a squelchy PLOP! and a second thing popped up, followed almost at once by a third.

"Waaah!" screamed Billy for the third time.

The first thing fixed him with its two beady eyes. *"Waaaah!"* it screeched. The other two joined in. *"Waaaah! Waaaah!"* they bellowed, grinning and nodding as they did so.

Terrified, Billy stepped back. "Wha' . . . wha' . . . wha' . . ." he said. He'd *wanted* to ask who they were, why they were there and what they were doing in his toilet. But the words wouldn't come.

"Wha'. Wha'. Wha'," the three things repeated cheerfully.

Then the third thing slipped. It grabbed the second thing, which grabbed the first thing, which lost its

balance, and all three of them toppled from the toilet and landed – with a CRASH! – on the floor.

If he hadn't been so frightened, Billy might have laughed. The three things climbed to their feet – all nine of them – and smoothed their belted tunics down with long tentacle-arms.

"I thought you said they could talk!" the first one said to the third.

"Yes," said the second angrily. "*Waaaah, waaaah, wha', wha'*! This language is unknown to me."

"It's an Earthling greeting," said the third knowingly. "I thought everyone knew that!"

As one, they turned to Billy. The purple and red blobs on their heads throbbed in unison.

"Can – you – speak?" they asked together; very slowly, very clearly.

"Y-y-y . . ." Billy stammered.

"You see," said the first thing triumphantly. "Not a word."

"Yes," Billy blurted out. "I can speak."

Surprised, all three things leaped backwards and trilled with delight.

"Greetings, Earth boy," said the first, raising a tentacle in salute. "We are the Blobheads of Blob. Second, third and . . . thirty-eighth wonders of the cosmos. My name is Kerek. This is Zerek. And that," he said with an airy wave of a tentacle, "is Derek."

"Greetings," said Zerek as he looked beneath the bathmat. "We seek the High Emperor of the Universe."

"We come in pieces," said Derek.

"We come in *peace*," said Kerek irritably.

Billy swallowed nervously. "G-good,"

he said. "But I don't think you'll find the High Emperor of the Universe here," he added.

The first Blobhead frowned. "This is the Barnes household, number 32 Beech Avenue, Winton Bassett, Earth, is it not?"

"Yes," said Billy uncertainly. "And I am Billy. But . . ." He'd been warned about talking to strangers – and they didn't come much stranger than the three Blobheads.

"Then this is the place," said Kerek. "The Great Computer is never wrong."

"The Great Computer?" said Billy.

Kerek nodded. "It—"

Before he could explain, Billy heard his dad calling from the hall. "Are you going to be much longer in there?"

"Nearly ready," Billy called back as Zerek and Derek trotted off to explore

. . . and experiment! They turned the taps full on, they squeezed tubes, they squirted aerosols . . .

"Who's that?" asked Kerek.

"My dad," Billy whispered.

Zerek replaced the toilet brush he had been sniffing and looked up. "One half of the production team which made him," he explained to Kerek and Derek.

"The female half," said Derek, who was busy nibbling the towels.

Billy smiled. "Actually it's— Oh, what!" he exclaimed as he noticed the state of the bathroom.

The basin was overflowing with bubbly water; there was toothpaste on the walls and hair gel in the bath; the forbidden medicine cabinet was open and empty, its contents floating in the growing pool of water on the floor.

"Stop it!" he yelled at the rummaging Blobheads. He turned off the taps, grabbed one of the shredded towels and began mopping up the sticky mess. "And don't just stand there!" he said. "Help me!"

"Billy?" His father was knocking at the bathroom door. "What are you up to?"

Billy gulped. "Nothing, Dad."

"Open the door, then," he said. "It's time for Silas's bath."

"Yes . . . I . . . Just coming . . ." He turned to the Blobheads. "What about you?" he whispered.

"Don't worry about us," Kerek whispered back. "Hyper-intelligent beings like us know how to blend in."

"We are masters of disguise," said Zerek.

"Morphtastic!" said Derek.

"Billy!" shouted his dad. "Open this door at once."

Billy had no choice. He slopped his way over to the door and slid the bolt across. His dad peered in.

"There's been a slight accident," he confessed. "There was this—"

"Waaaah!" screamed his dad. "I can see it!"

Billy spun round. Totally ignoring

16

the armchair and ironing board which had suddenly appeared in the middle of the floor, Mr Barnes stared at the giant purple and red cockroach in the bath. It was a monster, the size of a large dog. Its feelers trembled. "Waaaah!" it shrieked.

"*Waaaah!*" screamed Billy's dad even louder. He backed out of the room. "Billy get out of there," he said.

He turned and raced down the stairs. "I'll call the pest control people. The zoo. The police . . ."

Billy turned back, hands on hips. "Masters of disguise!" he said. "Morphtastic! Huh!"

The armchair, the ironing board and the cockroach became Kerek, Zerek and Derek again.

"Who is this *Silas?*" asked Kerek.

"He's my little brother," Billy explained.

As one, the three Blobheads' brains began pulsating with purple and red light. Six beady eyes narrowed. Nine stubby feet shuffled forwards.

"Take us to him," they demanded in unison.

Chapter Two

Silas was sitting in his cot banging on a small drum with his teddy. He looked up and gurgled.

Billy snorted. "Blobheads, Silas. Silas, Blobheads."

"Bobbolblobbolbobbobblob . . ." said Silas.

To Billy's surprise, instead of laughing, the three Blobheads fell on their knees.

"Oh, Most High Emperor of the Universe," said Kerek. "It is you."

19

"Bollobol," Silas giggled.

"Many *many* light-years," replied Zerek, nodding. "We used the alpha-gamma space–time wormhole."

"Blobbolobbolob."

"The *only* way to travel," said Derek.

Billy shook his head in amazement. "Are you telling me you can understand what he's saying?"

"The Most High Emperor's words are wise indeed," said Kerek.

Zerek reached inside the cot, wrapped his tentacles around Silas and pulled him out. "Right," he said, looking round furtively. "Let's be off, before someone else comes."

"Off?" Billy cried out. "What do you mean? And where are you going with my brother?"

Silas could certainly be a pain –

particularly since they shared a room – but seeing him being carried off by the Blobheads brought out all sorts of feelings Billy didn't even know he had. "Put him down!" he roared.

"Yes, put him down," said Kerek. "The wormhole portal isn't due back for another eleven minutes and eight seconds."

"But . . . this is crazy," said Billy. "Look at him. He can't possibly be the Most High anything of anywhere. He isn't even a year old yet."

"Or, to put it another way," said Kerek, "fifty dicrons old – as predicted in the *Book of Krud*. For, as it was written, 'You will know him by these signs. His nose will ooze greenness. He will smell of sour earth. A creature with unusually large ears will cover his chest.'"

"But that's just snot and poo," said Billy.

Zerek looked round anxiously. "Where?" he said.

"He's got a bit of a cold," Billy explained. "And his nappy needs changing."

"And the creature?" Kerek demanded.

"It's Randy Rat!" said Billy. "A cartoon character . . ."

"Blobbollobol," said Silas, and pointed at the rat on his T-shirt proudly.

"You see!" said Kerek triumphantly.

But Billy didn't see. "He's my brother, and he belongs here."

"Wrong!" said Kerek. "He is the Most High Emperor of the Universe and he belongs with us, on Blob."

"It's the only way we can keep him

safe," said Zerek, and shuddered.

"Safe from the wicked Followers of Sandra," said Derek.

"Sandra?" Billy snorted.

"You may well scoff," said Kerek, "but the Followers of Sandra are dangerous. They would stop at nothing to take the Most High Emperor for their own. And if *that* happened . . ."

All three Blobheads quivered from head to foot with a sound like jelly sloshing in a bucket.

"Who is this Sandra?" said Billy.

"Not *who*," said Kerek, "but *what*, for Sandra is a—"

"Enough of this," said Zerek, looking around nervously. "We really should be getting back to that wet room. We don't want to miss the return of the wormhole."

He picked up Silas again.

Billy raced across the room, grabbed his brother's legs and pulled. "Let him go!" he shouted.

Zerek wrapped his tentacles around Silas's chest and pulled back. "*You* let him go!"

"No, *you* let him go!"

"No, YOU let him go!"

"You can both let him go!" Kerek instructed. "How dare you treat the Most High Emperor of the Universe in such a manner!"

Silas giggled happily as Zerek and Billy lowered him gently to the carpet. "Bloboblob," he said.

Derek stepped forwards. "We have a problem," he said. "*We* need to take the Most High Emperor to the safety of Blob. *Billy*, here, wishes him to stay."

"Mum and Dad would blame me if he disappeared," he said. "I know they would."

"Precisely," said Derek. "So we must ensure that he doesn't disappear." He unclipped a small black box – one of many – from his belt and aimed it at Silas.

"Hey!" Billy cried in alarm. "What are you doing?"

"Solving our problem," said Derek. He tapped the box. "With my Meganostic Multi-Scan Gizmo. Just lock on the coordinates. And . . . pasta!"

The box emitted a blinding flash. Billy screwed his eyes shut. When he opened them again he couldn't believe what he saw. Where one snotty, smelly Silas had been sitting, now there were two.

"There!" said Derek. "Now everyone's happy. We'll take the original and you can keep the copy."

"No one will ever know the difference," said Kerek.

"And it's even got a clean nappy on," said Zerek hurriedly. "Now can we *please* depart, before—"

The box flashed a second time. Suddenly there were three Silases.

Again, and there were four.

Five. Six. Seven.

"Turn that thing off!" roared Kerek.

"I can't," said Derek, stabbing repeatedly at the box with his tentacle. "It's stuck!"

"That's all we need!" said Zerek dismally as a thirteenth Silas joined the rest. "And how are we supposed to tell which one is the *real* Most High Emperor of the Universe."

"Easy," said Kerek. "We sniff him out!"

Down in the hall, Billy's dad was having problems of his own. No one he called was impressed with his story of the giant cockroach. Not the pest control people. Not the zoo. And certainly not the police. He was calling the fire brigade when Mrs Barnes swept in through the front door.

"Meetings, meetings," she said, and blew her husband a kiss. "What's your day been like?"

Mr Barnes winced. "Hello?" he said. "Yes. I want to report a giant cockroach. It . . . Pardon? No, it's *not* on fire . . . What? Because I thought you could use your hoses to keep it at bay. I . . . Yes, just the one. But you

don't understand. It's colossal. The size of a pony—" The line went dead. ". . . at least," said Mr Barnes quietly. He turned to his wife. "She hung up," he said. "They all do."

"I'm not surprised," said Mrs Barnes. "A cockroach the size of a pony!" Her eyes narrowed. "What have you been cooking today?"

"Liver and Peach Roulade," said Mr Barnes proudly.

"Liver and . . . Oh, good grief!" Mrs Barnes exclaimed. "Are the children all right? Where are they anyway? Has Billy done his homework? Has Silas had his bath?"

"I . . . I . . ." Mr Barnes stammered.

"Oh, really!" Mrs Barnes snapped. "I get enough stress at work. The last thing I need when I get home is *more* stress! Giant cockroach indeed!"

"But there was," Mr Barnes said weakly.

Tutting impatiently, Mrs Barnes set off up the stairs. "Bil-ly! Si-las!" she called. "Mummy's home!"

The bedroom was overflowing with Silases by the time Derek finally managed to switch the machine off. Forty-seven in all there were – laughing, crying, crawling and dribbling, toddling and falling down. In amongst them were Kerek, Zerek and Derek – lifting, sniffing and replacing the babies, one after the other.

"He must be here somewhere!" said Kerek.

"But where?" said Zerek fretfully. "We'll never find him in time."

"Pfwoooarr!" said Derek, his blobby

30

head turning a shade of green. "I've found him."

At that moment, the door burst open. The Blobheads disguised themselves in an instant. Billy spun round.

"Mum!" he said.

"Billy!" she replied. "Silas." Her smile froze. "And Silas. And Silas. And Silas. And a watering can. And a toaster . . ." She closed her eyes and clutched her head. "Billy, love," she said. "Mum's had a very long day . . ." She opened her eyes again, and moaned.

The Silases were still everywhere. On the carpet. In the cot. And one in the arms of a gigantic fluffy blue kangaroo.

The room swam and Mrs Barnes fell to the floor in a dead faint. As she

landed, the watering can and toaster became Blobheads again. The fluffy blue kangaroo did not.

"Oh, Derek!" said Kerek and Zerek together.

"Sorry," said the kangaroo. It shrugged. "It happens."

"Yes, but always to you!" said Zerek furiously.

"All is not lost," said Derek. He stuffed Silas down inside his pouch and hopped towards the door. "Come on, you two," he said. "There isn't a moment to lose."

Chapter Three

Leaving his mum lying on the floor surrounded by the forty-six identical copies of Silas, Billy hurried after Zerek and Kerek and the fluffy blue kangaroo that was making off with his brother.

"Dad!" he yelled as he raced along the landing. "*Dad*!"

"Just a minute, Billy," he shouted back. "I'm on the phone . . . Hello? Is that the army?"

"But we haven't got a minute!" cried Billy. He raced to get to the bathroom door before the Blobheads could lock him out – and arrived just in time.

"Waaaah!" shrieked Zerek as the opening door propelled him across the slippery floor.

Kerek was looking down at a small black box of his own. "Ten seconds and counting," he said.

The fluffy blue kangaroo patted Silas down in his pouch and prepared to leap.

"Three . . . two . . . one . . ." said Kerek. "*Now!*"

The kangaroo leapt forwards into the toilet.

Billy gasped. He'd failed. The Blobheads were abducting his baby brother and there was nothing he could do to stop them.

"It's for the best," Kerek assured him.

"It's the only way," said Zerek.

"It's not here!" said the fluffy blue kangaroo.

"What?" screamed Kerek.

"The wormhole portal," said Derek. "It's not here."

"But it must be!" Zerek wailed. "How else are we going to get back?"

As Derek climbed out of the toilet bowl, Kerek inspected the screen on his small black box. "It makes no sense," he said. "The Great Computer stated that the wormhole would return to the same spot thirty minutes and nineteen seconds after—"

"No," said Zerek. "You're wrong. The confibulation matrix has quabbled, causing a tiny but significant difference in position. Five Earth metres to be precise. Which means . . ." He cocked his blobby head to one side. "Listen!"

From the other end of the landing, came a soft, swooshing *sucking* sound.

"That's *it*!" shouted Kerek. "To the bedroom at once!" And back they all ran.

"The size of an elephant, I tell you!" Billy heard his dad shouting down the phone. "Hello? Hello?"

They burst into the bedroom together: Kerek, Zerek, the fluffy blue kangaroo with Silas in its pouch, and Billy himself. Mrs Barnes, who was just coming round, raised her head, blinked twice, rolled her eyes and went out like a light once again.

"Look!" said Kerek, and pointed unnecessarily. They could all see the translucent tube swaying this way and that around the room, sucking copy

after copy of Silas in through its dark circular portal.

"It's already gone unstable," said Zerek nervously. "Four or five seconds more, and it'll be gone. Quick!" he screamed, and made a dash for the opening.

Unfortunately, Kerek and the kangaroo also had the same idea at exactly the same moment. The three of them – four, including Silas – ended up sprawled across the floor. Silas crawled out of the fluffy blue pouch.

"Blobberlobbolblob," he said, and pointed at the last of his twins as he too was sucked up inside the gleaming wormhole. Silas climbed to his feet and toddled after him.

"*No!*" bellowed Billy. He leaped forwards, grabbed Silas under the arms and pulled him away. Abruptly, the wormhole quivered, faded and disappeared.

Silas was outraged. His face turned purple, his eyes screwed shut, his mouth snapped open and he screamed and screamed.

"See what you've done?" Kerek said to Billy. "The Most High Emperor of the Universe is displeased."

Billy looked down at the little ball of rage. "One day he'll thank me," he said.

"And us?" said Zerek. "What is to become of us?" He turned on Derek. "This is all your fault!" he said.

"Mine?" said Derek, shaking his fluffy blue kangaroo's head. "Why?"

Silas screamed all the louder.

"Because it's *always* your fault!" yelled Zerek.

"Now, now, fellow Blobheads," said Kerek. "Squabbling is pointless. Let us see what the Great Computer has to say . . ."

"Waaaah!" screeched Silas. "*Waaaah!*"

Billy looked down at his mum. The noise was waking her up. Her eyelids were flickering. "She's coming round!" he whispered urgently. "And Dad's coming!" he added as he heard the sound of heavy feet pounding up the stairs.

"What do we do? What do we do?" squealed Zerek, spinning round and round.

"In the wardrobe, all of you," said Billy, pulling the door open for them.

Kerek nodded. "You won't betray us, will you?" he asked as he climbed in.

"Of course not," said Billy.

"We have ways of dealing with traitors," said Derek threateningly – or rather, as threateningly as it is possible for a giant fluffy blue kangaroo to be. As Derek pulled the wardrobe door shut, the door opposite flew open. Mr Barnes burst in. He saw his wife lying on the floor.

"Alison!" he cried, and raced to her

side. "What happened?"

Mrs Barnes sat up and looked round groggily. "Babies," she said. "Everywhere. And a gigantic fluffy blue kangaroo . . ."

"Bet it wasn't as big as that cockroach," he said.

Silas stopped screaming. "Blob blob," he said, and crawled past his mum and dad.

"Pfwoooarr!" said Mrs Barnes.

"I was just about to change his nappy," said Mr Barnes.

"*Silas!*" Billy yelled when he realized where his brother was heading. Straight towards the wardrobe!

Hadn't the Blobheads warned Billy that they must not be betrayed? With his heart in his mouth, he jumped forwards and made a grab for his little brother. But too late. Silas's pudgy hands were already tugging at the wardrobe door.

The hinges creaked. The door swung slowly open. Billy stared into the darkness inside – and gasped.

Chapter Four

"'Ello! 'Ello! 'Ello!" came a voice, and a short, fat policeman stepped out of the wardrobe and crossed the room to Billy's parents. "I understand you've been having a spot of bother with a giant cockroach," he said.

"Y-yes, Officer," said Mr Barnes as he climbed to his feet. "That's right. I . . ."

Mrs Barnes stared at the ludicrously small helmet wobbling about on the top of the policeman's enormous, *blobby* head. Her eyes narrowed. "What were you doing in that cupboard?" she demanded.

"Looking for clues," said the policeman. "I can tell you now that the said bug is not, and never has been, hiding there."

"But—" Mrs Barnes began.

"Don't worry, madam," the policeman said. "I'll soon get to the bottom

of this."

And with that, he hurried from the bedroom. As he did so, the wardrobe door opened for a second time.

"We've had an emergency call about a giant cockroach," said a tall, thin firefighter, dressed in a garish uniform the exact same colour as Mr Barnes's Lime and Anchovy Compote.

"Th-that was me," said Mr Barnes. "And thank you for coming so promptly."

"All in a day's work," the firefighter said. He slammed the wardrobe door shut. "You may rest assured that I shall not leave this house until the afore-mentioned creepy-crawly creature has been located and disposed of."

And so saying, he too made a speedy exit from the bedroom. Mr Barnes smiled sheepishly. "Good to see they

took my calls so seriously," he said.

At that moment, a noisy kerfuffle exploded from inside the cupboard. Mrs Barnes turned to her husband.

"Who else did you call?" she asked weakly.

"I . . . errm . . . Oh dear," he said.

"Well?"

"The army," he admitted.

Mrs Barnes groaned. "So I suppose

that's a soldier," she said. The frantic banging and crashing grew louder. "Or soldiers. It sounds as though there's a whole regiment of them in there!"

All eyes fell on the cupboard.

"Let me out!" came a muffled cry.

Mr and Mrs Barnes crossed the room and began tugging at the wardrobe door. Billy watched nervously.

"Let me out!" the voice cried again.

Mr and Mrs Barnes tugged at the door all the more desperately.

"*Let me ou*—!"

At that moment the catch clicked, the wardrobe door burst open and out sprung the gigantic fluffy blue kangaroo. Mr Barnes was sent flying. He landed on the floor with a loud CRASH! Mrs Barnes landed on top of him. And above them both towered

the fluffy blue kangaroo.

It looked down. "Sorry about that, madam, sir," it said. "I don't suppose either of you have seen a giant cockroach, have you?"

Mr Barnes shook his head. Mrs Barnes opened and shut her mouth, but could not speak.

"No matter," said the kangaroo as it bounded off towards the bedroom door. "You leave it all to me."

"You see!" screamed Mrs Barnes when it was gone. "I *told* you there was a kangaroo!"

Mr Barnes hugged his wife tightly. "I know you did. I . . ." He turned to Billy in desperation. "Do *you* know anything about all this?"

"Know about what?" he said, pretending to be puzzled.

"About *what*?" his dad exclaimed.

"About that gigantic fluffy blue kangaroo!" shrieked his mum.

Billy swallowed anxiously. He knew that no explanation would be good enough. "Gigantic fluffy blue kangaroo . . . ?" he said innocently. "What gigantic fluffy blue kangaroo?"

Chapter Five

"You both work too hard," said Billy sympathetically. "I'll tidy up in here and change Silas's nappy. You two go downstairs. Have a cup of Dad's dandelion and nettle tea. Put your feet up. Relax."

"Thank you, Billy," said his dad shakily. "I think we might just do that."

The moment Mr and Mrs Barnes had gone, Billy grabbed Silas and dashed back along the landing. "Where are you?" he hissed as loudly as he dared. "Kerek? Zerek?"

There was a noise from the bathroom. Billy went in. He saw the toilet seat slowly rising, and four beady eyes peek out.

"There you are!" he said. "Where's Derek?"

"Derek!" Kerek snorted. "Trust him to mess up. We'd have got away with it if it hadn't been for him."

"He's a disgrace!" said Zerek furiously.

"Never mind about all that," said Billy. "Where is he?"

At that moment, the shower curtain moved. Billy strode across the room and yanked it back.

"Waaah!" the kangaroo cried out – and abruptly turned back into a Blobhead. "*That* did the trick," he said. "I must have morphed because

you made me jump."

"Not as much as you made Mum and Dad jump," said Billy sternly.

Kerek frowned. "I can see we're going to have to be careful about our disguises."

"I had no idea humans were such timid creatures," Zerek sniffed.

"Grown-ups are," said Billy. "And if I know my mum and dad, it's going to take more than a cup of dandelion and nettle tea to calm them down."

"You're right," said Derek, stepping forwards. He handed Billy yet another of the small black boxes from his belt.

"What is it?" asked Billy suspiciously.

"It's a Positron Memory Massage Gizmo. One zap will remedy the situation," Kerek explained. "After all, if we're going to stay here . . ."

"You're staying?" Billy exclaimed.

"Until the wormhole returns," said Kerek.

"And when will that be?"

Kerek unclipped a small black box from his own belt and squinted down at the screen. "According to the Great Computer the next wormhole portal will be along again in another thirteen hours . . ."

He paused.

He frowned.

He rubbed a tentacle over his blobby head. "Or is that years?"

Zerek groaned. "Centuries, most like," he said. "Knowing *my* luck!"

Derek shuffled forwards and tickled Silas under the chin. "Perhaps it was

meant to be," he said. "After all, someone has to protect the Most High Emperor from the evil Followers of Sandra. It might as well be us."

Having tidied the room and changed Silas, as promised, Billy went downstairs. He found his parents sitting at the table in the kitchen. They looked awful.

His dad was hunched over with his head in his hands, his mum was staring unblinkingly at the wall. Before them, stood two steaming mugs of dandelion and nettle tea – untouched.

Billy looked down at the Positron Memory Massage Gizmo. "This had better work," he muttered. He took aim and fired. A dazzling bolt of light flew out across the room, swirled around his parents for a second – and disappeared.

Mrs Barnes looked up. "Fluffy blue kangaroo!" She smiled. "It's work. I've been under far too much stress recently."

"Of course you have," said Mr Barnes. "You need a break. We both do." He chuckled. "Giant cockroach indeed! It *must* have been something I ate!"

Billy sighed with relief. His parents were acting as though nothing had happened. At last the Blobheads had managed to come up with something that actually worked!

"All right, Mum, Dad?" he said brightly.

"Fine, thanks, Billy," said his dad as he rose several inches off his chair into the air. "I'm feeling *wonderful*."

Billy let out a soft, miserable groan. He might have known that there would be a hitch to the Blobhead's gizmo!

"Without a single care in the world," said his mum as she too floated dreamily up from the table.

"Good," said Billy nervously. "I . . . I'll just go and get Silas."

And with that he raced off to ask the Blobheads whether there was some little black box or other on their belts which would bring his parents back down to earth again.

"Oh, the side effects won't last long," Kerek assured him as roars of laughter and squeals of delight floated up from the kitchen.

Zerek glanced over at the bedroom clock. "In fact—"

At that moment, there was a loud

crash, followed by another. Mr and Mrs Barnes had come down at last – and with a bang!

Billy winced. "Uh-oh!" he said. "Is there anything you can do about a pair of badly bruised bottoms?"

"Of course!" said Kerek. "For we are the Blobheads of Blob. Second, third and . . ." he glanced at Derek, "ninety-third wonders of the cosmos. There is *nothing* we cannot do!"

Meanwhile, far, far away on the other side of the universe, in the outer reaches of the Spider Galaxy, the planet Blob circled its purple and red sun. It was a typical day. The sky was green. The air was stale. The clouds on the horizon suggested a slime-storm was imminent.

And at number 76, The Mouldings,

Vera and Zera – two elderly and, if truth be told, rather decrepit Blobheads – were wondering what on Blob they were going to do with the forty-six identical pink alien babies which had suddenly appeared in their bed chamber.

BLOBHEADS titles available
from Macmillan

Read all about the Blobheads' adventures!

---

1. Invasion of the Blobs	£2.99
2. Talking Toasters	£2.99
3. School Stinks	£2.99
4. Beware of the Babysitter	£2.99
5. Garglejuice	£2.99
6. Silly Billy	£2.99

All Macmillan titles can be ordered at your local bookshop
or are available by post from:

Book Service by Post
PO Box 29, Douglas, Isle of Man IM99 1BQ

Credit cards accepted. For details:
Telephone: 01624 675137
Fax: 01624 670923
E-mail: bookshop@enterprise.net

Free postage and packing in the UK.
Overseas customers: add £1 per book (paperback)
and £3 per book (hardback).

The prices shown below are correct at the time of going to press.
However, Macmillan Publishers reserve the right to show new retail
prices on covers which may differ from those previously advertised.